*For Clare*

This edition copyright © 2001
Baby's First Book Club®
Bristol, PA 19007
First published in Great Britain by HarperCollins Publishers Ltd in 2001

1 3 5 7 9 10 8 6 4 2
ISBN   1-58048-204-X

Text and illustrations copyright © Jez Alborough 2001
The author/illustrator asserts the moral right to be identified as the author/illustrator of the work.
A CIP catalogue record for this title is available from the British Library.

Printed in Hong Kong.

# Jez Alborough

# FIX-IT DUCK

Plop! goes the drip that drops in the cup.
Duck looks down and Duck looks up.

"A leak in the roof.
Oh, what bad luck!

This is a job for . . .

FIX-IT DUCK."

He says, "It's easy to repair."
But how's he going to reach up there?

He can't climb up—
it's much too steep.

So he drives round to borrow

a ladder from Sheep.

Over the puddles
he hops and he skips,

to Sheep's little house,
then, *OOPS*, he trips!

"Sheep!" calls Duck.
"It's only me."

And he explains how the rain
had dripped in his tea.

When he reaches the part about fixing the leak,
they hear a rattle, creak, and squeak.

"It's my window," says Sheep.
"It won't close. It's stuck."

"This is a job for
**FIX-IT DUCK.**"

He does what he can to close up the gap.
He glues it, screws it, and gives it a tap.

"The problem," says Duck, "is your glass is too thin."
"My house," wails Sheep. "The rain's coming in!"

"What we need," says Duck, with a glint in his eye,
"is to pull your house to somewhere dry.

Goat's got a shed. We can put it inside.
Let's hook up your Jeep and go for a ride.

Back up slowly,
till I say stop."

Then all of a sudden,
something goes *POP*!

"Flat tire!" says Duck. "More bad luck.
We'll have to use my pickup truck."

But Sheep's little house won't hitch to the truck.

"This is a job for ...          FIX-IT DUCK."

"We're off," says Duck as they speed down the track.

"Slow down on the bends," calls Sheep from the back.

Turn left," he bleats as they skid round a curve.
Hold on tight," quacks Duck as the truck starts to swerve.

And the house should follow behind but instead . . .

...it unhooks from the truck

and rolls on straight ahead.

When Duck gets to Goat's, he starts to explain
why they'd brought Sheep's house, which was letting in rain.

"But where is it?" asks Goat.
Then as Duck turns to see,

Frog runs up, shouting,
"It's following me!"

"Look up the hill,"
gasps Goat in dismay.

"It's Sheep," quacks Duck,
"and he's coming this way!"

'*Run!*" cries Frog.
'He's going to crash!"

"H - E - L - P !" bleats Sheep.

"It's broken," says Duck. "What a lot of bad luck."

"Oh, no!" moans Sheep, "*not* ... FIX-IT

If only he hadn't come calling on me.
If only that rain hadn't dripped in his tea."

DUCK!  "Not rain," says Frog, with a shy little cough.

"He forgot to turn his bathwater off."